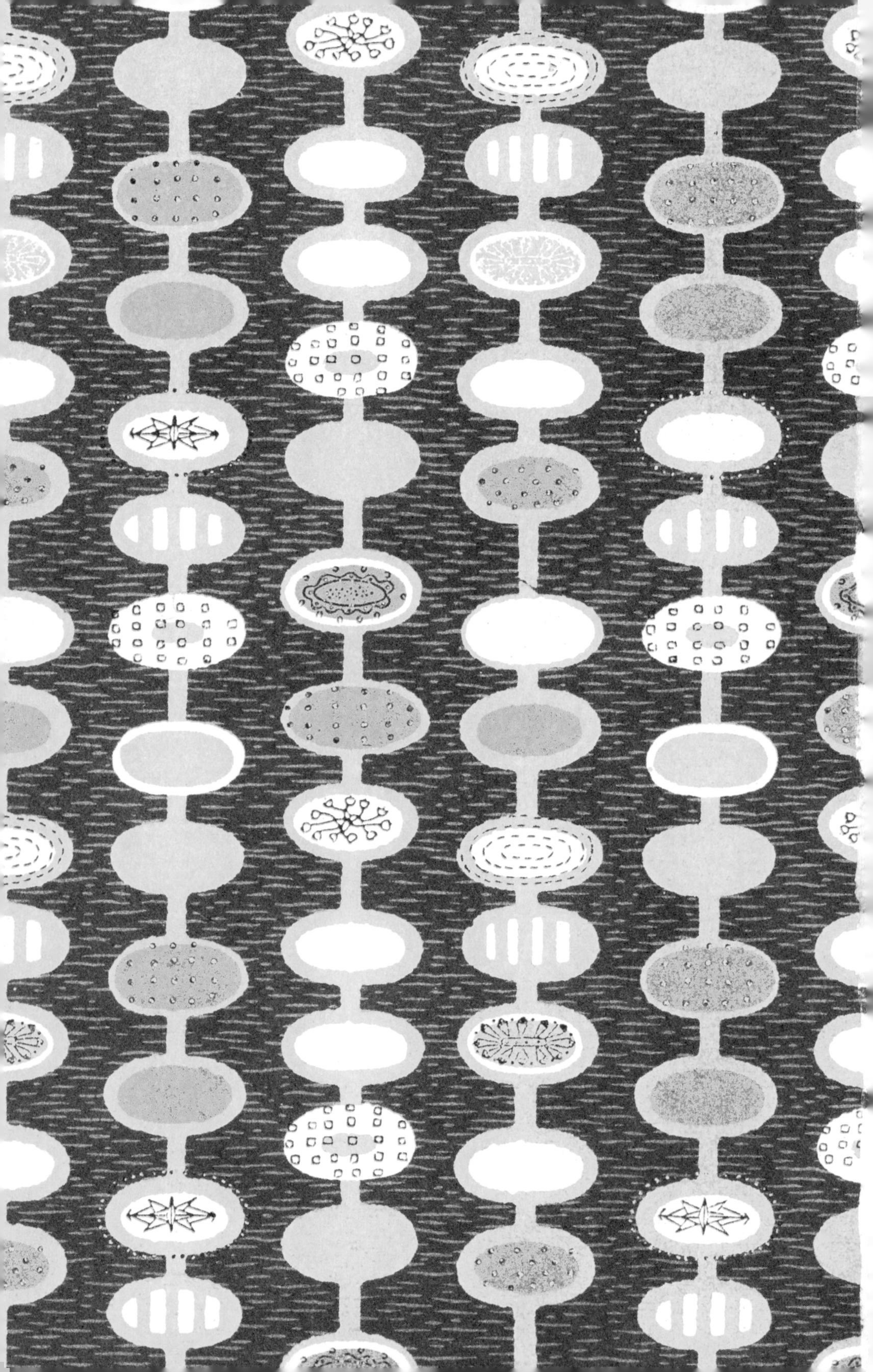

THE SCORE

IDW PUBLISHING

Ted Adams, CEO & Publisher
Greg Goldstein, President & COO
Robbie Robbins, EVP/Sr. Graphic Artist
Chris Ryall, Chief Creative Officer/Editor-in-Chief
Matthew Ruzicka, CPA, Chief Financial Officer
Alan Payne, VP of Sales

www.idwpublishing.com
ISBN: 978-1-61377-208-9
15 14 13 12 1 2 3 4

Become our fan on Facebook: facebook.com/idwpublishing
Follow us on Twitter: @idwpublishing
Check us out on YouTube: youtube.com/idwpublishing

RICHARD STARK'S PARKER: THE SCORE. JULY 2012. FIRST PRINTING.

IDW Publishing, a division of Idea and Design Works, LLC.
Editorial offices: 5080 Santa Fe St., San Diego, CA 92109.

PRINTED IN KOREA.

RICHARD STARK'S

PARKER

the Score

A Graphic Novel

BY

Darwyn Cooke

EDITED by SCOTT DUNBIER

IDW PUBLISHING

San Diego 2012

This one's for every poor son of a bitch that's ever had to work with me.

RICHARD STARK'S PARKER: 

Score

JERSEY C
TRAVELUX
THIS END UP
CITY
HA
in Bracer
OLICE
SOS
FIREH
QUAL
FD

TY 1964
LUX
BANK
DETER

BOOK ONE

MONDAY, APRIL 13

HOTEL

GAAH!!

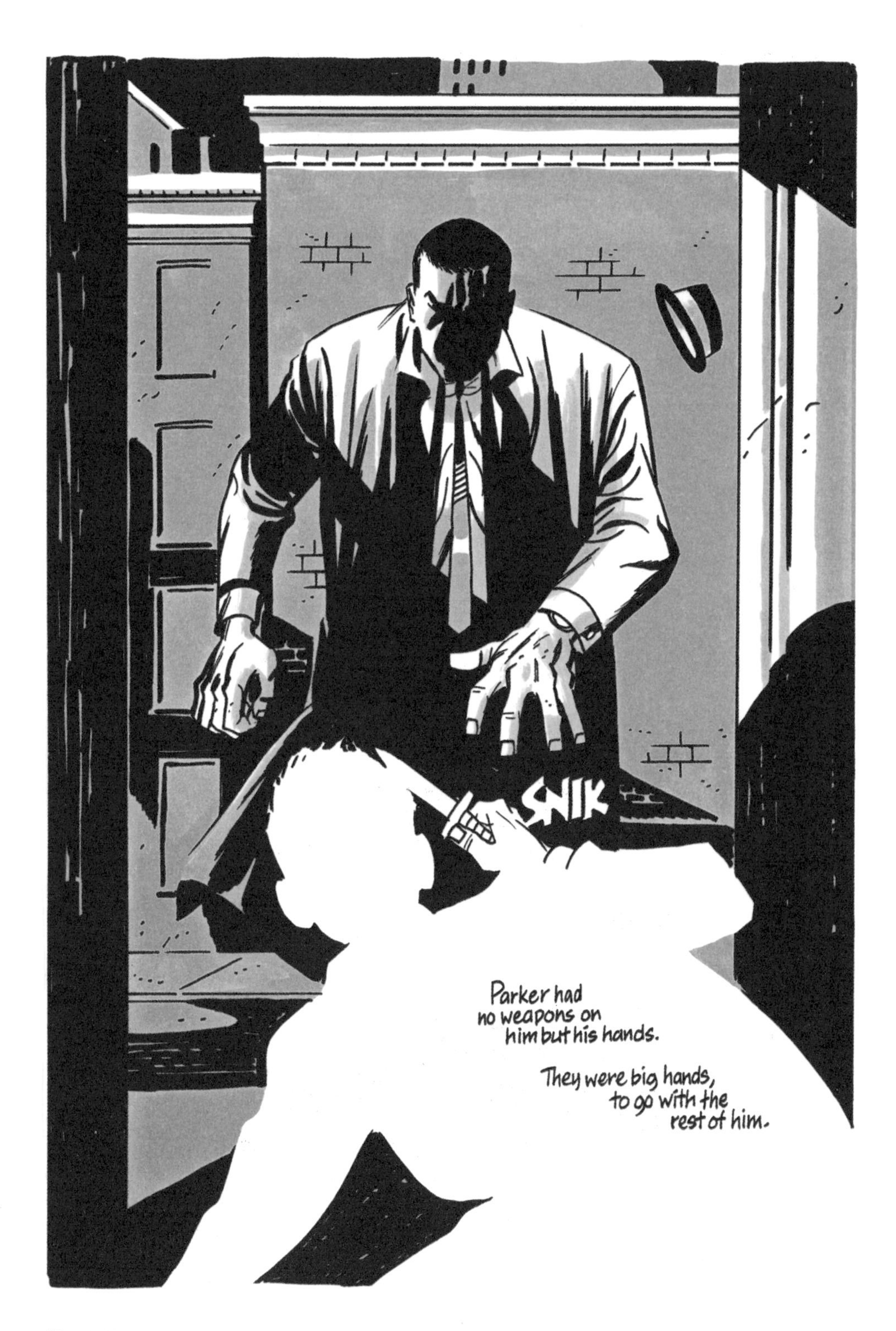
SNIK
Parker had no weapons on him but his hands.
They were big hands, to go with the rest of him.

KRÜNCH
HLACK

Dead?

Parker immediately regretted not pulling his punch. Why had he been following him?

Did he know about Paulus and the others? His pockets told Parker that his name was Edward Owen but little else.

STATE OF NEW YORK
Kleenex
LUCKY STRIKE

Parker took the wallet and money and cigarettes.
He left Owen in the alcove.

The job was sour.
He didn't know why, but he didn't need to.

He'd warn Paulus and then head back to Miami.

He'd been swimming when the call came.
Joe Sheer was passing on a message from Paulus about an upcoming job.
Parker hadn't needed the money, but it had been six months since he'd last worked. Inactivity, no matter how hedonistic, always brought him to this point.
It was boredom more than anything that had led him from the beach to Jersey City.

KNOCK
KNOCK

WELL, HEY. PARKER.

PAULUS

C'MON IN.
THE DEAL'S OFF.

WHAT?
SOMEONE WAS FOLLOWING ME.

OH, THAT. THAT DON'T MEAN ANYTHING.
HE'S DEAD.

YOU KILLED HIM? FOR CHRIST'S SAKE, WHY?
HE PULLED A KNIFE.

I DON'T KNOW, PARKER. THAT'S A HELL OF A THING.
TELL ME, PAULUS, HOW DID YOU KNOW I WAS FOLLOWED?

IT WAS EDGARS.
HE THOUGHT IT WAS A GOOD IDEA.

WHO THE HELL IS EDGARS?

YOU DON'T KNOW HIM. HE'S NEVER WORKED AN OPERATION LIKE THIS BEFORE.
THEN WHAT IS HE DOING HERE?
HE SET THIS UP.

AN AMATEUR?
GOODBYE, PAULUS.

PAULUS!

WHAT'S THE HOLDUP HERE?

EDGARS

EDGARS, THIS IS PARKER.
IT SEEMS THERE WAS SOME KIND OF MISUNDERSTANDING.
WHAT KIND OF MISUNDERSTANDING?

THE MAN YOU HAD TAIL ME PULLED A KNIFE.

THAT WAS STUPID. I DON'T CONDONE THAT. I'LL SPEAK WITH HIM.

NOT RIGHT AWAY, YOU WON'T.
TELL HIM, PAULUS.

OWEN IS DEAD.
DEAD?
YOU KILLED HIM?

JESUS. I HAD NO IDEA SOMETHING LIKE THIS WOULD HAPPEN.

I KNOW. SEE YOU, PAULUS.

HOLD ON -- WHERE THE HELL ARE YOU GOING?
I'M OUT.

WAIT.
WILL YOU WAIT A GODDAMN MINUTE?

WHAT FOR?
PAULUS, GO WAIT WITH THE OTHERS.

LOOK, YOU ... GENTLEMEN, YOU ALL KNOW EACH OTHER. KNOW WHAT TO EXPECT FROM EACH OTHER.
I DON'T KNOW ANY OF YOU AT ALL.

WHEN I'M AROUND YOU, MY BACK ITCHES.

SURE. WE AREN'T EXACTLY SAINTS. SO WHY GET INVOLVED?
A QUARTER OF A MILLION DOLLARS, FOR ONE THING.
AND PERSONAL REASONS.

YOU'VE GOT PAULUS AND THE REST. YOU DON'T NEED ME.
THEY TELL ME YOU'RE THE BEST.
THAT'S WHO WE NEED. THE VERY BEST.
SO WHY SHOULD I WORK WITH YOU?
FAIR QUESTION.
FIRST OFF, THIS IS A SPECIAL CASE. I PROMISE YOU THAT.
ALL THE MEN IN THAT ROOM SWEAR YOU'RE THE MAN TO RUN A CREW THIS SIZE.
I KNOW THIS IS A SOLID DEAL BUT I NEED A PRO TO TELL ME SO. JUST HEAR ME OUT.
WHO ELSE IS IN THERE WITH PAULUS?
TWO MEN. WYCZA AND GROFIELD.
THEY'RE GOOD MEN. SO YOU FIGURE IT'S A FIVE MAN JOB?
OH NO.
WE'RE JUST THE DEPARTMENT HEADS.

I FIGURE THIS JOB WILL NEED TWO DOZEN MEN.
MAYBE THIRTY.

YOU DON'T HAVE ANYTHING AT ALL.
IF A JOB TAKES MORE THAN FOUR OR FIVE MEN, IT'S NO JOB. YOU CAN PUT THAT DOWN AS A RULE.
YOU GOT AN OPERATION SET UP BY AN AMATEUR FOR PERSONAL REASONS. AMATEURS GET THEIR IDEAS FROM MOVIES AND PERSONAL REASONS GET IN THE WAY OF CLEAR THINKING.

SEE, THIS IS WHY WE NEED YOU.
C'MON, YOU TRAVELLED ALL THIS WAY. AT LEAST LISTEN TO THE PITCH. I'LL HAVE MY SAY AND THEN WE FOLLOW YOUR LEAD.
FAIR ENOUGH?

-sigh-

HAVE A SEAT.
I'LL GO GRAB SOME BEER AND WE'LL GET GOING.
ALL FOOLS IN A CIRCLE.
HA.

GROFIELD

HELLO, GROFIELD.
ARE YOU IN, PARKER?

WYCZA

I DON'T KNOW YET, DAN.
HERR EDGARS IS THE MYSTERIOUS TYPE, NO?
GENTLEMEN, CAN YOU COME IN HERE?

MINE
MAIN STREET
PPSST
HIWAY 22A
← STATE TROOPERS

GENTLEMEN.
THIS IS COPPER CANYON, NORTH DAKOTA.
BANK
POLICE
SAY WHAT YOU WILL, THE MAN HAS TALENT.
SHUT UP, GROFIELD.

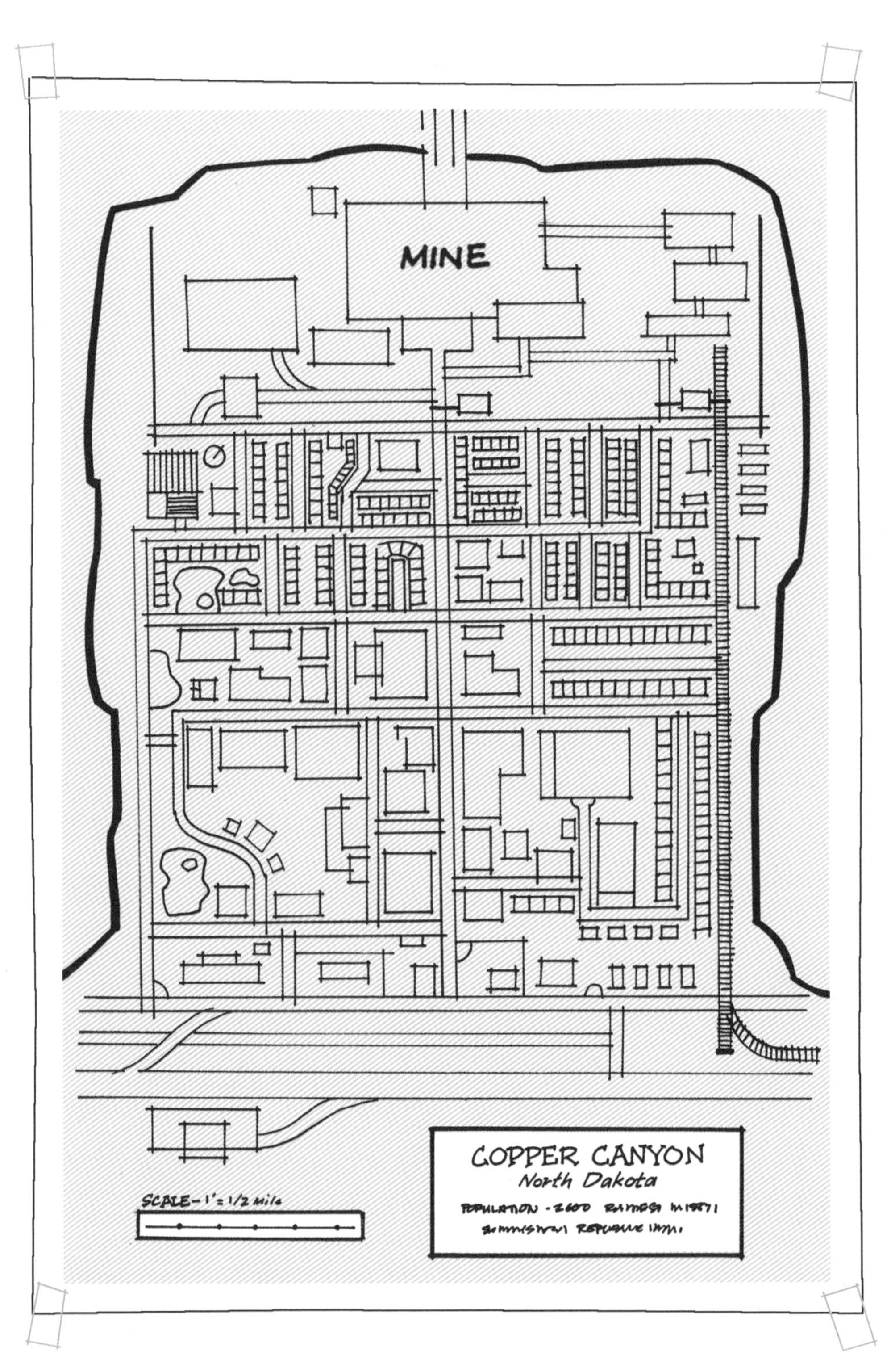
MINE
COPPER CANYON
North Dakota
SCALE - 1' = 1/2 Mile

IF YOU LOOK AT THE MAP, YOU CAN SEE A WAVY LINE SURROUNDING THE CITY.
THOSE ARE CLIFFS. THE CITY IS BUILT INSIDE A BOX CANYON, TOO STEEP AND TALL TO BE PASSABLE.

THE ONLY WAY IN OR OUT OF TOWN IS HERE ON THE OPEN SIDE OF THE CANYON.
THAT'S STATE HIGHWAY 22A.

COPPER CANYON IS A ONE INDUSTRY TOWN -- COPPER. THE REFINERY AND THE MINE ARE AT THE BACK OF THE CANYON. THERE ARE TWELVE BUILDINGS TOTAL.

THE WHOLE THING IS SURROUNDED BY STORM FENCING WITH TWO GATES.
ARMED GUARDS, DAY AND NIGHT.

IN TOWN, THERE ARE TWO BANKS, HERE AND HERE.
THE PHONE COMPANY IS HERE.
POLICE HERE.
POLICE

OVER HERE WE HAVE NATIONWIDE FINANCE AND DOWN MAIN THERE ARE THREE JEWELRY STORES.

Edgars droned on, touring them through his cardboard town. Parker waited for him to get to the point.

Then suddenly, he got it.

YOU'RE CRAZY.

AM I?

SWEET JESUS.

HEY, WAIT A MINUTE --

HA. FANTASTIC.

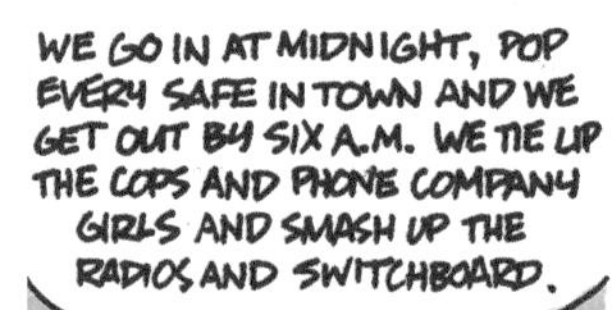
WE GO IN AT MIDNIGHT, POP EVERY SAFE IN TOWN AND WE GET OUT BY SIX A.M. WE TIE UP THE COPS AND PHONE COMPANY GIRLS AND SMASH UP THE RADIOS AND SWITCHBOARD.

PHONE COMPANY

WE GET AWAY USING THE STATE HIGHWAY. YOU ADD UP THE MINE PAYROLL WITH THE BANKS, JEWELERS, LOAN COMPANY AND DEPARTMENT STORES, THE TAKE SHOULD TOP A QUARTER OF A MILLION.

WELL FUCK ME GENTLY.

It was science fiction. The operation broke too many rules. Set up by an amateur. Requiring too many men. Involving going into a box with only one way out. But the idea pulled at Parker. The size of the challenge and the size of the take kept him from closing the door entirely.
They left Edgars to his tabletop town and agreed to meet again the following night. Parker caught a ride with Wycza and Grofield. They sat with coffee and talked it out.
DINER
Grofield waxed romantic.
STANLEY KRAMER
"IT'S A MAD, MAD, MAD, MAD WORLD"
the biggest entertainment ever to rock the screen with laughter
SPENCER TRACY
MILTON BERLE
SID CAESAR
BUDDY HACKETT
ETHEL MERMAN
MICKEY ROONEY
DICK SHAWN
PHIL SILVERS
TERRY-THOMAS
JONATHAN WINTERS
JIMMY DURANTE
I MEAN, THERE'S THE MONEY, OF COURSE. THEN, THERE'S THE SHEER DARING OF SUCH AN OPERATION.
TUNN
DINE
TELEPHONE
STEAK
ICE COLD D

IF IT COULD BE DONE AT ALL, IT WOULD BE FASCINATING.
I DON'T LIKE THAT TROOPER BARRACKS TWO MILES DOWN THE HIGHWAY.
THE ONLY WAY OUT OF THAT BOX IS RIGHT PAST THEM.

FIRST THINGS FIRST. LET'S TALK ABOUT MANPOWER.
I SEE FOUR MEN ON STATIONARY PLANT THE ENTIRE TIME.

ONE AT THE POLICE STATION. ONE AT THE PHONE COMPANY. AND ONE AT THE MINE OFFICE. THEY CAN HANDLE INCOMING CALLS AND THE LIKE.
WE PUT THE FOURTH IN A PARKED CAR ON THE TOWN LINE TO WARN US IF WE HAVE UNEXPECTED GUESTS.

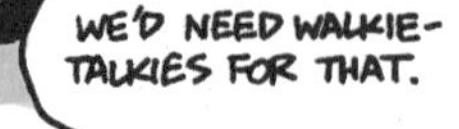

WE'D NEED WALKIE-TALKIES FOR THAT.
THEY'RE CHEAP, IN ANY SURPLUS STORE.

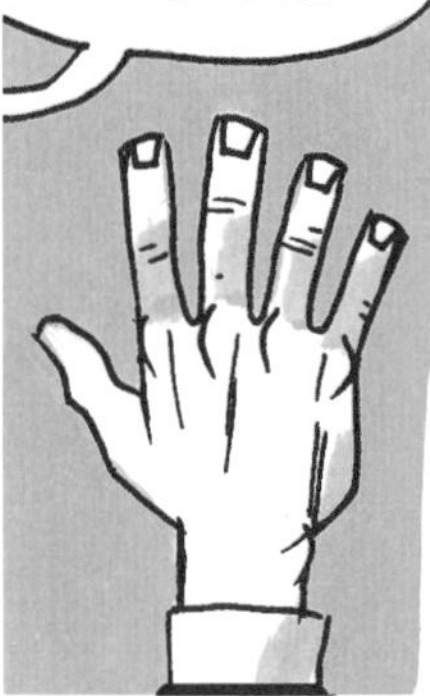
FIVE MEN HIT THE POLICE STATION. ONE STAYS.

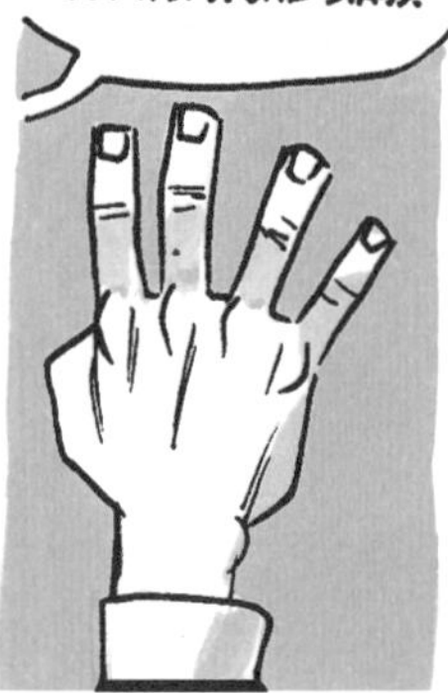
THAT LEAVES FOUR TO HIT THE PHONE COMPANY. ONE STAYS.

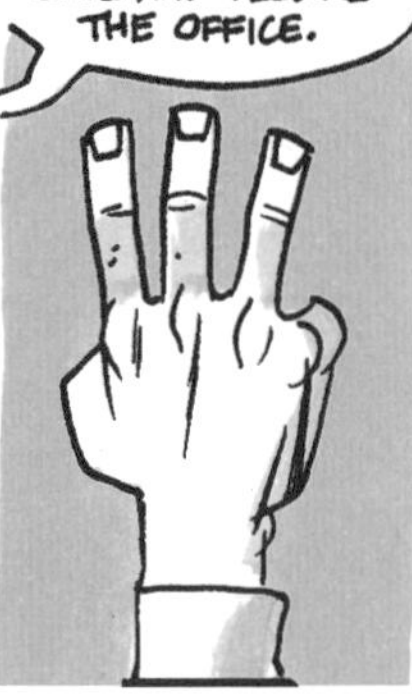
THE FINAL THREE HIT THE MINE'S MAIN GATE AND SECURE THE OFFICE.

THAT BRINGS US TO SIX.

EVERYTHING ELSE EDGARS WANTS TO HIT IS ON MAIN STREET. WE'D NEED FOUR MEN FOR THAT.
TWO BOX MEN, EACH ON ONE SIDE OF THE STREET WITH A PARTNER TO CARRY BACK THE LOOT.
TEN MEN TOTAL. SURE BEATS TWENTY-FIVE. SO WE'RE DOING THIS?
NOT ME. AT LEAST, NOT YET. WE NEED A GETAWAY PLAN. I'M NOT DRIVING FOUR CARS PAST THE STATE POLICE BARRACKS AT SIX A.M. PAYDAY MORNING.
EXACTLY.
I WANT TO SEE A HIDEOUT WE CAN GET TO BUT THE LAW CAN'T.

HOW ABOUT THAT LITTLE TOWN HE BUILT? KINDA NUTTY, RIGHT?
I FOUND HIS ENTHUSIASM AND CREATIVITY REFRESHING.

Parker left them there and headed back to his hotel. A whole goddamn town. It was a fairy tale, but he couldn't let it go.
NEL
VER

TUESDAY, APRIL 14
PSSSTT

GENTLEMEN! A TOAST TO A SUCCESSFUL VENTURE.

SETTLE DOWN, HERR EDGARS.
THERE ARE STILL A LOT OF SMALL THINGS TO FIGURE OUT. LIKE THE FIRE DEPARTMENT.

SHIT. I HADN'T THOUGHT OF THAT.
THAT MEANS ANOTHER MAN TO COVER THE FIREHOUSE.

HANG ON -- HOW ABOUT A DIVERSION? WE COULD START A BIG FIRE IN A QUIET CORNER OF TOWN TO KEEP THEM BUSY.

JESUS, GROFIELD, USE YOUR HEAD. A SIX HOUR FIRE?
WE NEED AN ELEVENTH MAN.

ACTUALLY, DAN, WE NEED TWELVE. I WANT A ROVER, SOMEONE WHO CAN TROUBLESHOOT UNEXPECTED BUSINESS AND BACK UP THE OTHERS.
SO IT'S TWELVE NOW.
TWELVE ISN'T SO BAD.
WE MAY NEED MORE. WHAT OTHER NIGHT PEOPLE ARE THERE?
NONE. THE ENTIRE TOWN IS ON A CURFEW. THEY ROLL UP THE SIDE-WALKS AT TEN O'CLOCK.
CURFEW. THAT WORKS IN OUR FAVOR.
I STILL DON'T LIKE THAT STATE POLICE BARRACKS.
RIGHT. OUR GETAWAY. AFTER YOU LEFT LAST NIGHT I PULLED OUT SOME TOPOGRAPHIC MAPS.
COME LOOK.
WHAT ARE WE LOOKING AT HERE?
THIS IS A GEOLOGICAL SURVEY MAP. THE AREA AROUND COPPER CANYON IS LITTERED WITH MINES AND COAL PITS.
THE COAL PITS GET SET UP AND WORKED UNTIL THEY PLAY OUT. SEE THIS 'X' I'VE MARKED?

FIFTEEN MILES ON THE 22A. THREE MILES ON THE SECONDARY ROAD, THEN IT'S ABOUT... SIX MILES IN ON THE MINING ROAD. SO TWENTY-FOUR MILES TOTAL.

Parker lingered in front of the map.
Twelve men. In at midnight, out by six in the morning.
From what he could see, if Edgars had his facts straight, they had everything covered.
It was a job. It would work.
It looked like science fiction at first, but it would work.
LUX
BANK
POLICE

BOOK TWO

WEDNESDAY, APRIL 15

PLEASE-
WAIT IN
HERE.
BE A PAL
AND RUB MY
BACK,
DROP
DEAD.
YOU BEEN
HERE BEFORE,
HAVEN'T
YOU?
NOT IN
YEARS.
AH, MR. GROFIELD.
HOW ARE YOU TODAY?
OH, DOC! THANK
GOD YOU'RE HERE.
I'VE GOT
THIS TERRIBLE
PAIN IN MY
BACK.
REALLY?
WELL THEN,
LET'S TAKE...
...A LOOK.
YOUR BACK IS
FINE, ISN'T IT?
HA!
AH, DOC,
YOU'RE
PRICELESS!
SHUT
UP,
GROFIELD.
DO I
KNOW
YOU?
THAT'S
PARKER.
HE GOT A
NEW FACE.

PARKER? I WOULDN'T HAVE KNOWN IT WAS YOU. IT'S GOOD WORK.
SO, YOU'RE NOT HERE ABOUT YOUR BACK. WHAT'S THE DEAL?
THE DEAL IS FOUR GRAND.
FOUR THOUSAND? WHAT, ARE YOU TAKING DOWN FORT KNOX?
SOMETHING LIKE THAT. WE'LL NEED IT SOON AS POSSIBLE.
SLOW DOWN, GROFIELD. IT'S A LOT OF MONEY FOR ONE OPERATION.
ARE YOU IN, PARKER?
I'M IN.
VERY WELL.
IT'LL TAKE A DAY OR TWO TO PULL THAT MUCH CASH TOGETHER. COME BACK THURSDAY AFTER TWO P.M.
ANYTHING ELSE?
JUST THIS TERRIBLE BACK PAIN. YA GOTTA HELP ME, DOC.
PLEASE FUCK OFF UNTIL THURSDAY, GROFIELD. GOOD TO SEE YOU, PARKER.
SLAM
Parker waited for Grofield to get over it.
HA HA HA HA HA HA

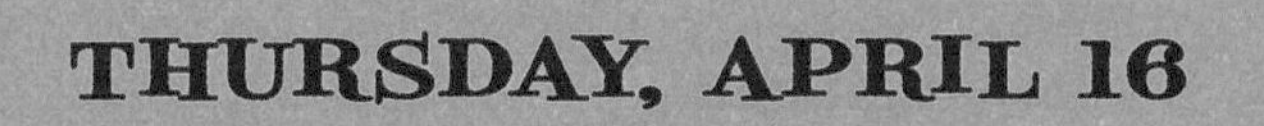

They had run up a list of men to work the job. Most were in the New York area but some came from as far away as Las Vegas and Kentucky.

Handy McKay was the only one to say no.

The dining room was packed with them and even with the windows open the room was full of smoke.

Paulus, Parker and Edgars laid it out.

They all had questions.

WHAT'S THE SPLIT?
WISS

EVEN ALL THE WAY. I KNOW IT ISN'T THE USUAL WAY, BUT THIS AIN'T A USUAL JOB.
I FIGURE 250,000 MINIMUM. SO 20K PLUS PER MAN.

WHAT ABOUT FINANCING?
PALM

FOUR GRAND. GOT IT TODAY.
THAT'S EIGHT BACK.
THAT'S A BIG BITE.
IT'S A BIG JOB, PALM.

HOW LONG WE GOTTA STAY AT THIS MINE?
ELKINS

'TIL IT COOLS. PROBABLY THREE OR FOUR DAYS.
I HATE THE FUCKIN' COUNTRY. OH, WELL.

WHAT IF THEM STATE BOYS THROW OUT ONE OF THEM HELIO-COPTORS?
HELICOPTERS.
WE'LL BE FINE. THERE ARE TWO LARGE WORK SHEDS AND WE CAN HIDE THE TRUCK IN THE RAVINE.
CHAMBERS

ALARMS?
CHO

MINE
THAT'S THE BEAUTY OF IT. THE WHOLE TOWN IS WIRED TO THE POLICE STATION.
NO BELLS OR ALARMS--JUST A BLINKING LIGHT AT THE COP SHOP.
WHEN DO WE DO THIS?
SALSA

AS SOON AS WE'RE SET. HOPEFULLY NEXT WEEK. IT HAS TO BE A THURSDAY IF WE WANT THE PAYROLL.
I SEE.

SO WE'RE DOING THIS? HOW ABOUT YOU, POP? YOU AIN'T SAID A THING.
ARE YOU IN?

INDUBITABLY.
'POP' PHILLIPS

IS THAT A YES?
THAT'S A YES, PAL.

They all wanted more beer.

Parker broke it down.
Paulus, you and Wiss run out to Copper Canyon and case all the secondary targets.
main st. Jewelery
WE'LL SELL INSURANCE. I'VE DONE THIS BEFORE, WISS. I GOT FAKE BROCHURES AND CARDS. WE DO A BAD JOB SELLING INSURANCE AND IN BETWEEN WE LOOK AROUND.
Wycza, you and Salsa go out there and look the copper mine over. No cameras--just make notes. And stay in a motel outside of town.
GOT IT.
SI.
Chambers, you get us a truck, right? The biggest one they make.
THAT'S THE ONE I'LL GET.
Cho, get a list together with Wiss and Paulus of what you'll need to blow the safes. Elkins will help you with it.
OH, SO I GET TO WORK WITH THE CHINAMAN?
I'M KOREAN, ASSHOLE.
KLUNK

Palm, you take Pops and a car out there and get a room outside of town. Start moving water and food out to the hideout. Make sure the sheds will hold our cars.
WE'LL NEED TWELVE COTS, TOO.
ARMY NAVY SURPLUS CEN
Grofield, you make sure everyone's got financing for their part, then pick up four walkie-talkies. Buy them up here.
ROGER THAT, MON CAPITAINE.
We need copies of the street maps with targets marked and any notes we can use. Twelve sets, done by hand. That's you, Edgars.
GOOD, GOOD.
WHAT ABOUT YOU, PARKER?
WHAT'LL YOU BE DOING?
GUNS.

FRIDAY, APRIL 17
MACHINE GUNS?
THEY'RE EXPENSIVE, MACHINE GUNS.
HOBBYLAND
AURORA
Revell
PRIVATE
VATE

THE GOVERNMENT TRIES TO KEEP TABS ON THEM.

TOUGH TO FIND ONE WITHOUT A HISTORY.

I NEED THREE.
AND THREE RIFLES.
AND EIGHT HANDGUNS.

158 IN KIT FORM
FERRARI F1 OP
SLOT-O-RACING
RIFLES, HANDGUNS, NO PROBLEM. MACHINE GUNS, THAT'S A PROBLEM.
I NEED THREE.
SIT. SIT, SIT. LET ME THINK.

YOU KNOW WHAT THE GERMANS CALL A MACHINE GUN? *Kugelspritz.* BULLET SQUIRTER.
NO ACCURACY.
THREE.

I GOT A SCHMEISSER, AN OLD BURP GUN -- GOOD CONDITION.
THAT'S ONE.
PARKER, PARKER. I HEARD YOU GOT A NEW FACE, BUT YOUR VOICE DON'T CHANGE, OR YOUR STYLE.

YOU DON'T LIKE ME, DO YOU, PARKER?
I DON'T GIVE A DAMN ABOUT YOU.

YOU DON'T LIKE THE DIRTY OLD BLIND MAN. HE SMELLS BAD.
YAH, PARKER?

MAYBE I'LL GO SEE AMOS KLEE.
FOR MACHINE GUNS? NO, PARKER, FOR MACHINE GUNS YOU COME TO ME.
YOU COME TO SCOFE.

SO TAKE A LOOK AT THE BURP. OVER THERE IS A TABLE WITH BATTLESHIP MODELS. BRING ME THE BOTTOM LEFT BOX.

JUST GIVE ME A SECOND.
I COULD PUT THIS TOGETHER BLINDFOLDED.
-SNORT-

CHAK
CHIK CHAK
CLICK

THERE.
YOU LIKE IT?
IT'S OKAY. LEAVE IT OUT.

WHAT ELSE HAVE YOU GOT?

YOU TAKE THE BURP, I CAN GIVE YOU TWO TOMMYS, ONE HUNDRED A PIECE.
THERE ARE SIX ROAD RACER SETS UNDER THE TABLE. BRING ME THE FORTH AND FIFTH BOXES.

I'LL TAKE THREE OF THESE.
THOSE TWO ARE ALL I GOT.
ROAD

THEN I WANT TO BUY ANOTHER ROAD RACER SET. THE ONE ON THE BOTTOM.

YOU'RE A BASTARD, PARKER.
YOU'RE A ROTTEN BASTARD!
A FILTHY, ROTTEN SON OF A BITCH!

YOU TAKE ADVANTAGE OF AN OLD BLIND MAN --
-- YOU'D SPIT ON YOUR MOTHER!

YOU'RE A CESSPOOL, A WALKING CESSPOOL!
YOU'RE VOMIT!
A CHEAP, ROTTEN PUNK!

SHUT UP, SCOFE.
I DON'T LIKE TO DEAL WITH YOU. YOU SMELL BAD.
THREE TOMMYS. HOW MUCH?

I HATE YOU. HATE YOU LIKE POISON.
THREE FIFTY.
SCOFE--
DEAL.

YOU'RE ALL RIGHT, PARKER.
YOU DON'T MEAN ALL THOSE THINGS YOU SAY TO ME.

GOODBYE, SCOFE.
WHAT ABOUT THE OTHER STUFF?
FORGET IT.
YOU'RE GOING TO KLEE?

YOU ROTTEN SON OF A BITCH!
SCUM! VOMIT! CESSPOOL!

PARKER?
Parker paid the woman out front and pointed his car toward Syracuse. The added trip to see Klee was going to eat an extra day.

SUNDAY, APRIL 19
THIS IS JEAN. SHE'S WITH ME.
SINCE WHEN?
SINCE ALWAYS.
Parker looked at her.
She wouldn't be with anybody always, especially not Edgars.
LOOK
STEVE MCQUEEN
SO WHAT?
SO SHE'LL BE COMING ALONG.
NO DICE.
RELAX, PARKER. SHE'LL STAY OUT OF THE WAY.
SHE'LL STAY OUT OF THE WAY A HELL OF A LOT BETTER RIGHT HERE.

PARKER, I GIVE YOU MY WORD--

I DON'T WANT YOUR WORD. SHE'S NOT COMING ALONG.

COULD YOU BASTARDS AT LEAST LOWER YOUR VOICES? YOU TALK ABOUT ME LIKE I'M NOT EVEN HERE AND IT'S GOT ME IRRITATED.

WHO'S THE BOSS AROUND HERE, HONEY?
NOBODY.
THAT'S JUST THE KIND OF TROUBLE YOU BRING WITH YOU.

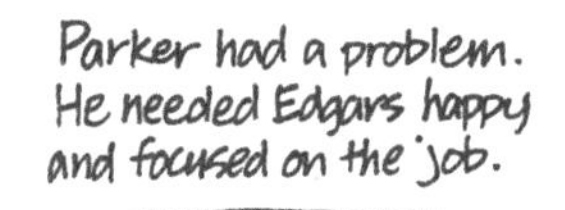
Parker had a problem. He needed Edgars happy and focused on the job.

SHE'LL STAY IN A HOTEL ON THE OTHER SIDE OF THE STATE LINE.

ALL RIGHT. GET PACKED.
GOOD! YOU HAVE TO GET HOME AND PACK.
ALERT! ALERT!

YOU CAN DRIVE ME.
TAKE A CAB.
YOU'RE THE ONE IN A HURRY, UGLY.

FINE. GET IN THE CAR.
GREAT. I'LL BE READY WHEN YOU GET BACK.

She was making an effort, so he ought to make an effort too. He concentrated, and his face relaxed.

She was available. Any other time, he'd probably do something about it. He had no appetite for women when he was on the job.
He built himself a drink instead.
HEY, UGLY!
YOU WANT TO DRY MY BACK?
YOU DO IT.
ARE YOU AND EDGARS FRIENDS OR SOMETHING?
I TRY TO BE NICE, AND YOU PUT ME DOWN. WHAT'S THE MATTER WITH YOU?
MAYBE AFTER.
YOU MEAN AFTER THIS BIG SECRET MISSION YOU AND CHARMING BILLY GOT ON?
SOMETHING LIKE THAT.
NOW HURRY UP.
Ten Minutes Later --
WELL?
DO I GET A GOLD STAR?
YEAH.
SURE. GOLD STAR MOTHER. I HAD A BOY IN THE SERVICE, BUT HE DIED.
C'MON, UGLY, BE A GENTLEMAN AND BRING MY BAGS.

MONDAY, APRIL 20
They dropped the girl in a small town called Thief River Falls and crossed the state line.
THERE IT IS.
HOW FAR IN?
ABOUT SIX MILES.
GOOD ROAD.
CHRIST, IT'S HOT FOR APRIL.

The trunk was full of guns. There were the three Thompson machine guns from Scofe and Amos Klee had come through with three rifles and eight handguns. Assorted shells sat stacked in assorted boxes.
RIGHT HERE.

OKAY, NOW THIS IS ROUGH ROAD.
0 10 20 30 40 50 60 70
PRNDL1L2
LET'S SEE HOW FAST WE CAN DRIVE IT.
SO THIRTY-FIVE, TOPS.
WHAT'S WITH THE TREES?
SULPHUR KILLS 'EM.

PARKER. YOU MADE GOOD TIME.
PALM.
YOU CAN PARK IT IN THERE WITH THE REST OF THEM.
GOOD.
GOOD, GOOD.
COME ON OVER AND CHECK OUT THE LIVING QUARTERS.
WE'RE STILL WAITING FOR CHO, CHAMBERS AND ELKINS.
HEY GUYS. ARE YOU HUNGRY?
HELLO, PAULUS.
GIMME TWO.

IT LOOKS GOOD, HUH, PARKER?
IT'S OKAY.

MAY AS WELL GET COMFORTABLE. IT'S HOME FOR THE NEXT WHILE.

HOW'S IT LOOK IN TOWN?
GOOD.

SEE ANY PROBLEM WITH GOING THURSDAY?
NONE. IT'S PIE ON THE SILL.

SOMEONE COMING.

CHO AND ELKINS. I'LL GET THEM SITUATED.
LET ME SHOW YOU THE WALKIE-TALKIES.

FOUR UNITS-- I HAD THEM SET UP SO ANYTHING SAID THROUGH ONE IS HEARD BY ALL THE OTHERS.
PERFECT.
PLEASE TELL ME YOU GUYS GOT SOME BEER.
ELKINS. CHO.
YOU GUYS HUNGRY?
HEY, PAULUS. I NEED A COOL PLACE TO STORE THE JUICE.
THE BEER?
OVER HERE, ELKINS. SIT IN FOR ME WHILE I SHOW CHO WHERE TO STORE THE NITRO.
WE DO IT THIS THURSDAY?
RIGHT. I FIGURE A WEEK IS ALL WE'LL BE ABLE TO TAKE OF THIS PLACE.
WE'RE SET, HUH? THIS IS LIKE I TOLD YOU, RIGHT?
IT'S FINE.

HERE COMES CHAMBERS.
O-VRRR
RRRRRRR
KSSSSS
CHAMBERS.
PARKER.
NICE TRUCK.
YEAH, IT'S A BIG BASTARD.
WHERE DO I PUT HER?
DOWN THERE.

YOU GOTTA BE KIDDING.
ORE TRUCKS DID IT.
HEAVIER TRUCKS WITH LOW CENTERS OF GRAVITY. WE GOT US ONE TALL, EMPTY TRAILER BACK THERE.
SHE WANTS TO RUN.
SHE WANTS TO FLY DOWN THIS GODDAMN HILL!

NO PROBLEM.
YOU'RE GOOD.
SHIT! HOLD ON.
MOTHER.
PARK UNDER THAT OUTCROPPING.
KSSSS

IT'S TOO SHINY. WE'LL GET SOME BLACK PAINT FOR THE TRAILER.
BROWN. LIKE CAMIO-FLAGE.
RIGHT. BROWN.
SMELL THAT? LIKE ROTTEN EGGS.
SULPHUR FROM THE MINE. MAKES THE WATER LOOK LIKE WINE.
SHIT, THAT'S NASTY.
SO NOW WE GET TO WALK BACK UP?
RIGHT.
CHRIST, PARKER--

WE MAY AS WELL BE WORKING FOR A LIVING.

THURSDAY, APRIL 23
11:30 P.M.

CHECK.
SI.
COPY.
COPY.

VVVVVRRRRROOOM

When they made the mine road Chambers killed the lights. It was over six miles to the secondary road and they did it at a crawl.

Chambers strained to see by what light the stars gave him. Beside him, Parker lit a cigarette and sat quiet.

The last few minutes before a job, he was always quiet, almost in suspended animation.

He had no imagination for the few hours ahead, nor worry, nor anything else. His consciousness worked at the level of recording the jouncing truck cab and the feel of the smoke and the darkness beyond the glass.

BOOK THREE

Grofield
heard background music.

Sometimes lush and full, with a lot of strings.
Sometimes rapid fire, that busy-street-with-yellow-taxicabs music.
Sometimes strident, harsh and dramatic.
ALOON
But always music, in the air around his head like a halo.

Right now the music was sharp staccato drumbeats, sparsely laced with a plaintive trumpet.
This made perfect sense since Grofield and his squad were trapped in an enemy town.

CLEAR?
CLEAR.

BIG DOG, THIS IS BRAVO ONE - WE ARE MOVING ON THESE NAZI BASTARDS.

WRAP IT UP, GROFIELD.

TIME TO GET SERIOUS.
POLICE

Officers Felder and Mason rolled down Raymond Avenue, looking for people violating the curfew. Mason wanted to pull over for a cigarette.
POLICE

OFFICER FELDER, OFFICER MASON, COME IN.
OLD FRED'S GETTIN' HIGH-FALUTIN'.

HE'S JUST KIDDIN' AROUND.
YES SIR, OFFICER NIEMAN, WHAT CAN WE DO FOR YOU, SIR?

COME IN TO THE STATION. SOMETHING'S COME UP.
WHAT'S THAT?
JUST GET IN HERE. OUT.

SOMETHING'S GOT OLD FRED IN A TWIST. WE'D BEST HEAD IN THERE.

HUH.
A BROWN TRUCK. FUNNY COLOR FOR A TRUCK.

Paulus sat on the floor of the truck in the dark. Sitting there, while actions important to him were going on outside, was torture.

Wycza's cigar flared and Paulus tried not to fidget in the dim light.

POLICE

HELLO, OFFICER NIEMAN.
YEAH, FRED, WHAT'S THE BIG DEAL?
I'M SORRY, BOYS.

SORRY? C'MON FRED, DON'T FUCK AROUND.
AL--

Mason's brain scrambled to catch up with his eyes.
EITHER OF YOU MAKE A MOVE, YOU'RE DEAD SEVEN TIMES.

Mason thought, a war attack. Commies!
PUT YOUR GUNS ON THE COUNTER AND TELL US YOUR NAMES.
ALBERT F-FELDER.
A-AL.
JIM MASON.
Or maybe worse.

ALL RIGHT, JIM, AL-- WHO'S GOT THE CAR KEYS?
UH, ME. I DO.
PUT THEM ON THE COUNTER.
NOW BOTH OF YOU GET BACK THERE WITH FRED.

LISTEN CLOSE.
FOR THE NEXT FEW HOURS YOU'VE GOT NOTHING TO DO BUT WAIT.
DON'T GET CUTE AND YOU'LL BE ALL RIGHT.

Sorry, fred-
we didn't get it.

DIDN'T GET WHAT?

SON OF A BITCH!

YOU HEAR WHAT HE TRIED TO PULL?

IT NEVER WORKS.
YOU OKAY, FRED?
YOU ANSWER HIM NOW, BOY. DOUBLE QUICK!
I-I'M OKAY.

GET INTO YOUR CHAIR, FRED.
AL AND JIM, I NEED YOU TO LIE FACE DOWN ON THE FLOOR. WE'RE JUST GOING TO TIE YOU UP.

They tied and gagged Mason and Felder, then rolled them under the command counter. Past Felder's head, Mason could see them.

Mason thought the voice he was hearing was familiar. He listened as the other men's footsteps receded to nothing.

All of a sudden Mason knew and his terror doubled.

Salsa sat in a stolen car, cool and collected.
SALSA? YOU SET?

SET. I'M IN A BLACK DODGE ON RAYMOND AVENUE, FACING OUT, ONE BLOCK IN FROM THAT WELCOME SIGN.

ANYBODY COME IN SINCE US?
NOT IN OR OUT.

ALL RIGHT. WYCZA?

HERE.

WE GOT THE POLICE STATION. GOING AFTER THE FIREHOUSE NOW. IF YOU SEE THE PROWL CAR, DON'T WORRY, I'LL BE THE ONE DRIVING IT.

HA! WANT US TO START NOW?

WAIT UNTIL WE'VE GOT THE FIREHOUSE AND PHONE COMPANY LOOKED AFTER.

RIGHT.
I'LL LET YOU KNOW.

Chambers felt good. All the nervousness was gone, all the jumpiness out of his system. From the second he'd clubbed that smart-ass cop, every bit of jitters washed out of him.
FIRE
POLICE
C'MON, PARKER. LET'S ROLL.
DON'T HIT THEM, CHAMBERS. WATCH THEM IF THEY BEHAVE, SHOOT THEM IF THEY DON'T. NOTHING IN BETWEEN.
I'M GOOD NOW, PARKER. LET'S JUST ROLL.
ALL RIGHT.
Chambers moved to the left of the door and sensed Parker moving to the right. This was the part he liked, moving fast and moving sure, moving like the pieces of a clock.
FIRE

PROMISE YOU WILL HELP
PREVENT FOREST FIRES!
STEP AWAY FROM THE DESK.

I NEED BOTH OF YOU MEN TO TRY AND STAY CALM. WHAT ARE YOUR NAMES?

While Parker gave them the spiel, using their first names a lot, telling them how nothing would happen to them if they didn't try nothing stupid, Chambers plunked down in a chair.
He kept his rifle level and hoped one of these bastards would make a run for it.

He wasn't so sure about Parker. What was all this crap about first names? Who cared what kind of first names these stupes had?

They tied all the firemen up in the bunkhouse and left Chambers with an old guy named George.

WHAT ARE YOU PEOPLE GOING TO DO?

CURIOSITY KILLED THE CAT, GEORGE.
Nothing to do but wait. Chambers hated waiting. He found himself wishing he was on truck detail.

It had fallen to Grofield and his ragtag group to knock out the Axis radio towers.

WELL, THIS IS IT, SARGE.
?

From the halls of Montezuma--

AMERICAN TELEPHONE & TELEGRAPH CO.
BELL SYSTEM
AND ASSOCIATED COMPANIES
COPPER CANYON BRANCH
347 WHITTIER
SHUT UP, GROFIELD.

Grofield had worked with Parker enough to know his methods. He was an expert with groups.
1 TERRIFY THEM SPEECHLESS

2 GROUP THEM TOGETHER
PLEASE MOVE TO THE MIDDLE OF THE ROOM.
3 PERSONALIZE THE MOMENT
YOUR DESKPLATE SAYS MRS. SAWYER. WHAT'S YOUR FIRST NAME?
EDITH.

4 GIVE THEM A MINUTE TO ABSORB AND GRASP THE SITUATION
INTRODUCE ME TO THE OTHER LADIES, EDITH.
I DON'T SEE WHY--
I'M LINDA PETERS.
M-MARY DEEGAN.
TRY AND STAY CALM, LADIES. NONE OF US WANTS TO HURT YOU.
Grofield had to laugh.

To see Parker before a job, or after, you'd think he was just a silent heavy, about as subtle as a gorilla.
GO TO HELL.

But on the job, dealing with any people that might be in the way, he was all psychology.
I'M SORRY, LADIES.

He was explaining it to them now, telling them he was sorry that two of them had to be tied and gagged. They were hanging on his words.

There was a lunchroom down the hall and they did their best to make the women comfortable. Parker and the rest left Grofield to his solo act.
NOW, MARY, I NEED YOU TO WRITE DOWN SOME PHONE NUMBERS FOR ME.
I'LL NEED A PAD AND PEN OUT OF THE DESK DRAWER.
IS THAT ALL RIGHT?
YOU DON'T HAVE A GUN IN THAT DRAWER AND IF YOU DO, YOU HAVE MORE SENSE THAN TO SHOW IT TO ME. GO AHEAD.

I NEED NUMBERS FOR THE POLICE STATION, THE FIREHOUSE, AND THE NIGHT PHONE AT THE COPPER MINE.
CAN I USE THIS? OR DO YOU HAVE TO DO SOMETHING THERE?
YOU CAN USE IT.
HELLO FRED? PUT MY FRIEND WITH THE GUN ON.
E? G HERE AT THE PHONE COMPANY. EVERYTHING'S FINE. YOU CAN REACH ME AT 7-3060.
7-3060
FIREHOUSE? LET ME SPEAK TO MY MASKED FRIEND.
C? G HERE. EVERYTHING'S COOL. THE NUMBER HERE...
SO MARY, DO YOU FOLKS HAVE DIRECT DIALING OUT HERE?
NOT YET.
IF ANYBODY WANTS TO CALL OUT THEY HAVE TO GO THROUGH YOU, RIGHT?
YES.

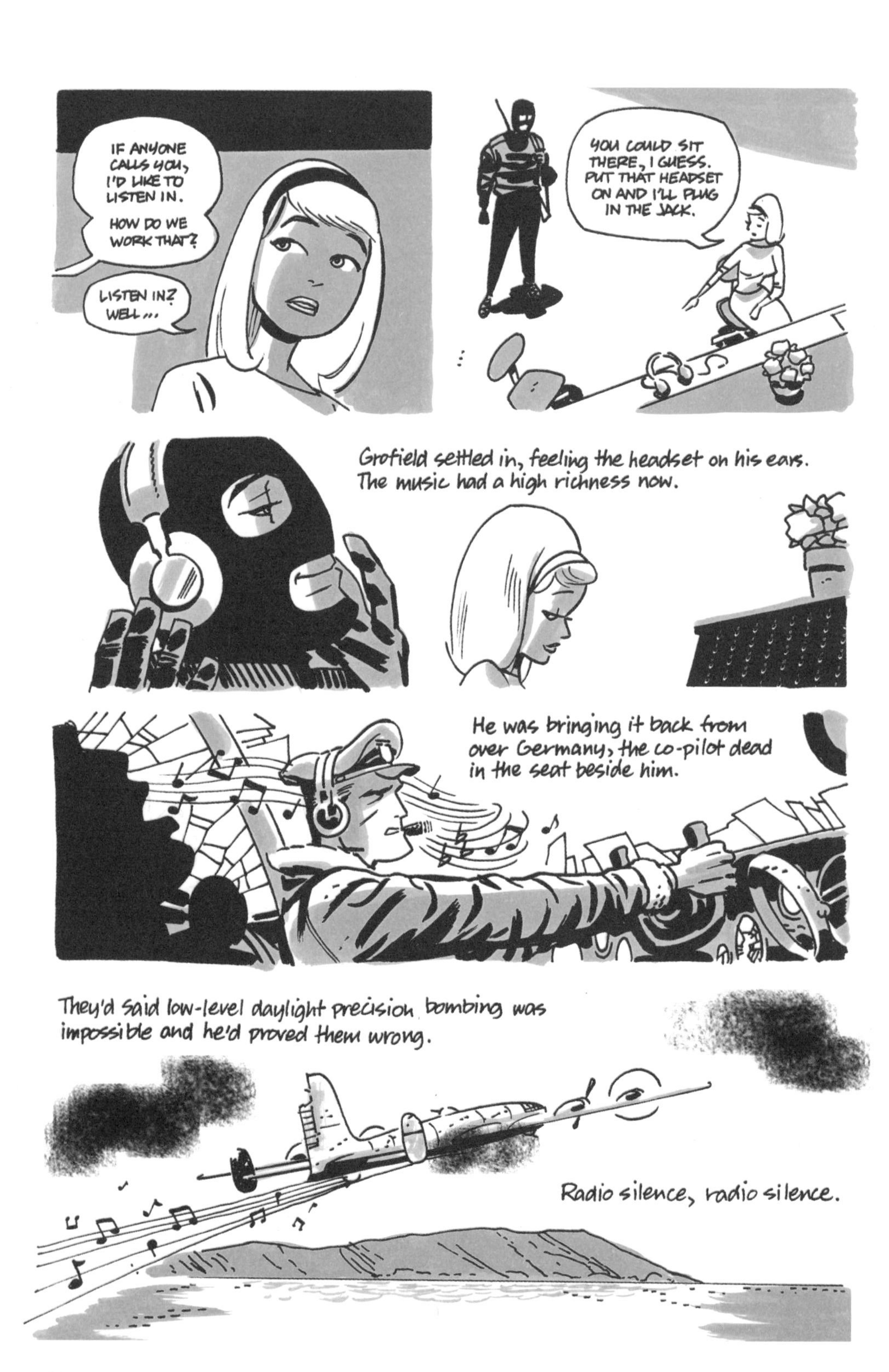
IF ANYONE CALLS YOU, I'D LIKE TO LISTEN IN.
HOW DO WE WORK THAT?
LISTEN IN? WELL...
YOU COULD SIT THERE, I GUESS. PUT THAT HEADSET ON AND I'LL PLUG IN THE JACK.
Grofield settled in, feeling the headset on his ears. The music had a high richness now.
He was bringing it back from over Germany, the co-pilot dead in the seat beside him.
They'd said low-level daylight precision bombing was impossible and he'd proved them wrong.
Radio silence, radio silence.

Wiss stood lookout. He didn't want any part of wrecking the radio station.
WCPR
POLICE

He liked machinery. He liked to tinker with it and learn how it worked. He couldn't stand to see it smashed.
It was the same way with his work. Wiss used a drill and a wrench and his own two hands.

As far as Wiss was concerned, men who used nitro were bums and amateurs, not professional safe men.

CLEAR?
CLEAR.

Wiss and Palm followed Parker and Phillips in the wagon. The mine squatted fat at the end of Main Street.
KL
POLICE

WE SHOULD PLAY A GAME.
RADIO STATION TAKEN CARE OF. NOBODY WAS THERE.
SHOULD WE START?
WAIT UNTIL WE GET THE WEST GATE.
YOU'RE GOING TO STEAL THE PAYROLL, AREN'T YOU?

ASK ME NO QUESTIONS, I'LL TELL YOU NO LIES.
WHAT DO YOU SAY WE PLAY TWENTY QUESTIONS?

I'M THINKING OF SOMETHING MINERAL.

I'M--I'M SORRY--

IT'S JUST MY NERVES.

IT'S OKAY, MARY.
IT'S JUST STAGE FRIGHT. DON'T WORRY ABOUT IT.

Parker stopped at the plant gate and the guard emerged. This part had no effect on Wiss at all.
POLICE
People were just fuses; Men like Phillips and Palm and Parker deactivated the fuses so men like Wiss could work.
It took two minutes for Parker and Phillips to "deactivate" the security guard. Then they were heading in to the main office.
Phillips' comical salute and fake moustache were lost on Wiss. His mind was on the box.
PLEASE BE SURE TO SIGN IN AT THE MAIN OFFICE, GENTLEMEN.

Palm covered the front office and called in to Grofield. Parker led Wiss to the back room with the payroll safe.

NO WINDOWS.
SO?

SO WE CAN USE THE LIGHTS.
RIGHT.

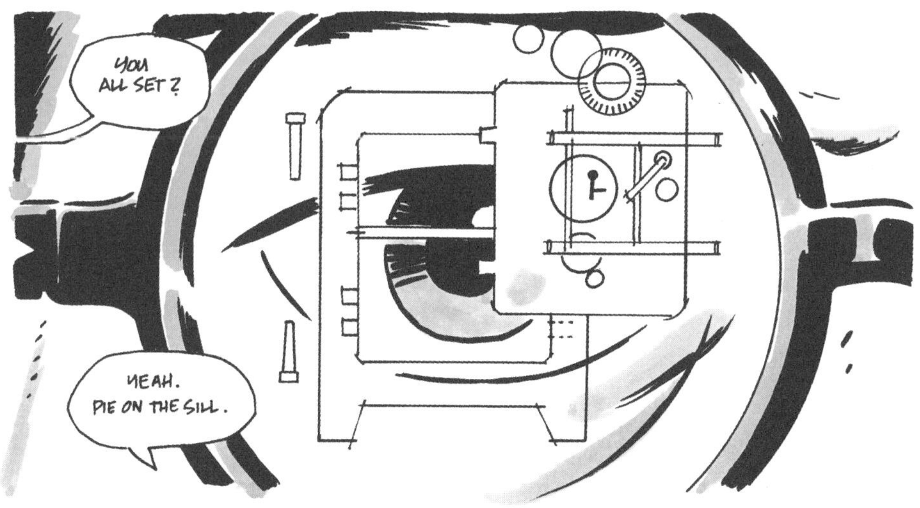
YOU ALL SET?
YEAH. PIE ON THE SILL.

WE GOT THE EAST GATE. YOU CAN START NOW.
OPEN 'ER UP.
Finally, thought Paulus. He was anxious from being cooped up in the dark.

SHEE-IT! IT'S A GHOST TOWN.

Paulus gulped the cool night air.
GIMME A SECOND, WYCZA.

They split into teams to tackle the safes. First up for Paulus and Wycza: Merchant's Bank.
LET ME GET THE DOOR.

HANG ON. LET ME GIVE US SOME LIGHT.

I CAN'T WORK IN THIS DAMN THING.

OVER THERE.
BINGO.

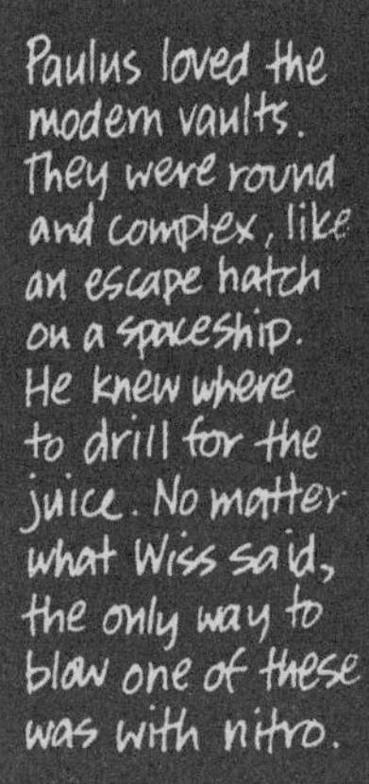
Paulus loved the modern vaults. They were round and complex, like an escape hatch on a spaceship. He knew where to drill for the juice. No matter what Wiss said, the only way to blow one of these was with nitro.

FIND ME AN OUTLET.

OVER HERE.
DO I NEED THE EXTENSION?

NO. HANDY, HUH? THE ARCHITECT HAD YOU IN MIND.

GOOD OF HIM.
VVRRRRR

Eddie Wheeler was scared. He'd missed the curfew. Betty Campbell's parents were away until Sunday.

He'd fallen asleep in her arms and when he finally woke up, Betty's clock said one.

He'd left Betty in the doorway and sprinted down Whittier toward Main street. Near Main he began to hear a high-pitched sound.

APPLIANC
Someone was robbing the bank! He had to warn the police somehow.

The problem was he'd catch it for missing the curfew.
DANG IT.

HELLO, POLICE? THIS IS EDDIE WHEELER. THERE'S A ROBBERY AT THE MERCHANT'S BANK!
HOLD THE LINE, SIR.

WHERE ARE YOU?
I'M IN THE PHONE BOOTH ON WHITTIER, NEAR RAYMOND.
STAY PUT. A CAR'S ON ITS WAY.

Three minutes later, the prowl car arrived.
OVER HERE! THEY'RE AT THE MERCHANT'S!

YOU OUGHT TO KNOW BETTER THAN TO BE OUT THIS LATE, EDDIE.

OH, CRAP. YOU'RE IN ON IT.

WALK DOWN WHITTIER, EDDIE. AHEAD OF ME.
DO LIKE YOU'RE TOLD AND YOU WON'T GET HURT.

I DON'T WANT TO KILL YOU, EDDIE. I GOT NOTHING AGAINST YOU. I'M GOING TO TIE AND GAG YOU, AND IN THE MORNING SOME PERSON WILL FIND YOU SAFE AND SOUND.
BUT IF YOU TRY ANYTHING CUTE, I'LL HAVE TO KILL YOU.

IN THERE.

WHAT ARE YOU DOING OUT PAST CURFEW, EDDIE?

I WISH I KNEW.

1:00
A.M.

2:00 A.M.
EDDIE WHEELER
CHAMBERS
COLEMAN'S
the Department Store
ELKINS
CHO
PARKER
SALSA
FOUR BLOCKS SOUTH

PALM
WISS
PHILLIPS
EDGARS
GROFIELD
AND
MARY
JOHANSEN
CREDIT JEWELERS
WYCZA
PAULUS

THIS IS W-- YOU THERE, P?
THIS IS P. WHAT'S UP?
EVERYTHING'S OPEN. WE'LL BE DONE LOADING IN ABOUT TWENTY MINUTES.
S, YOU HEAR THAT?
I DO-- THAT IS VERY GOOD NEWS.
G, YOU THERE?
G?
SHIT!
G? COME IN--
G HERE.
SPREAD THE WORD. WE LEAVE IN TWENTY.
RIGHT.

I DON'T SEE WHY I CAN'T COME WITH YOU.
JUST GIVE ME A MINUTE.
I DON'T WANT YOU TO FEEL THREATENED ABOUT IT. IF YOU LEAVE I'LL NEVER SAY A WORD ABOUT YOU TO ANYONE. I JUST WANT TO GO WITH YOU... UH... "G."
ALAN. MY NAME'S ALAN.
NOW LET ME DO MY JOB.
HELLO?
PUT E ON THE LINE.
POLI
THEY'RE ALMOST FINISHED. BE READY TO LEAVE IN FIFTEEN MINUTES.
GOT IT. FIFTEEN MINUTES.
ALMOST DONE HERE, FRED.

I WON'T BE NEEDING THIS THING ANYMORE.
EDGARS?
SURPRISE.
DON'T WORRY, BOYS. I DIDN'T FORGET ABOUT YOU DOWN THERE.
I'VE GOT YOURS RIGHT HERE.

CLICK
CLICK
CLICK
ARMO
ARMORY

FIREHOUSE? PUT C ON.
THIS IS C. WHAT'S THE WORD?
IT'S RUNNING FASTER THAN WE THOUGHT. WE LEAVE IN FIFTEEN.
BOY, YOU'LL NEVER KNOW HOW--
HEY,--
OH, NO!
CHAMBERS? CHAMBERS!!
P!
LISTEN-- SOMETHING'S GONE WRONG.
THE FIREHOUSE. IT SOUNDED LIKE MACHINE-GUN FIRE. WE WERE CUT OFF.

W, DO YOU HEAR THAT?
I HEAR IT.
TAKE THE WAGON. MEET ME THERE.
POLICE
WHAT THE HELL?!
WHAT HAPPENED?
POLICE
I DON'T KNOW. LET'S ASK EDGARS.
WE GOTTA GET OUT OF HERE.
I KNOW.
POLICE
JESUS, WHAT A MESS.
EDGARS...
WHAT'S HE SAYING?
CHIEF OF POLICE.
EDGARS USED TO BE THE POLICE CHIEF HERE.

They'd never proved anything on him, the bastards. Brutality? Kickbacks? You needed witnesses, you needed proof. He wasn't dumb enough to get caught by these hicks, not in a million years.
MINE
BANK
FIRE
POLIC
JEWELER'S
They couldn't return a single indictment, not a one. Fifty charges and not one indictment.
POLICE
FIRE
So they threw him out. The call to the mayor's office, the whole crowd there demanding he resign.
MIN
He refused, of course. The city council held a vote, and he was dismissed.
MINE

They ran him out of town. He swore to them they'd regret it.

They were about to find out he was a man of his word.

GOODBYE, COPPER CANYON.
I'LL BURN YOU TO THE GROUND!

Next was the mine. They were going to learn what it meant to cross him.

WHAT WAS THAT?
THEY MUST BE BLOWING A VAULT.
HOLD YOUR POSITION.

He knew every inch of this plant. Knew just where a grenade would do the most damage.

DANGE
NO SMOKIN
FLAMMAB

WHAT THE HELL IS GOING ON?
NOTHING! JUST HOLD YOUR POSITION.

nomee
Ekonomee Gas had a rail spur with a fuel car behind it. The perfect spot for the last grenade.

STOP!

EDGARS! STOP!
OLICE

STAND BACK, BOYS!

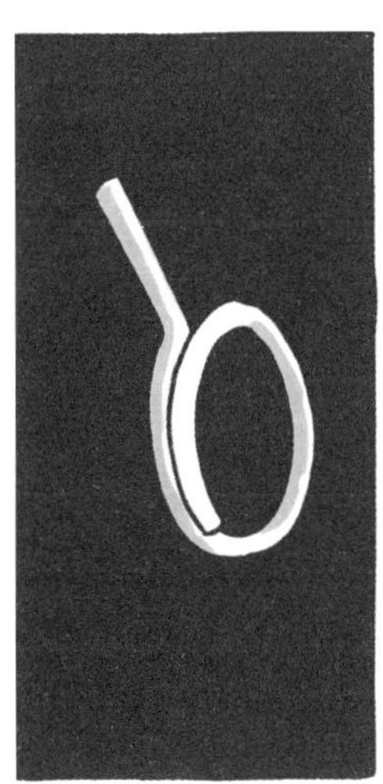

Wycza wrestled on occasion and he rolled with the blast.
The second explosion was another matter.
GOD...
DAMN.
EDGARS?
IN THERE.
G--CALL PALM--TELL HIM TO GET TO THE EAST GATE AND GET YOURSELF DOWNSTAIRS.
WHAT'S GOING ON?
LATER.
S, WATCH THE ROAD. IF THE TROOPERS DO COME IN. DON'T STOP THEM, JUST WARN US.
WILL DO.

I NEVER DID LIKE THAT TROOPER BARRACKS.

IT'S SOUR, PARKER. IT'S GONE SOUR.
I KNOW. YOU DRIVE THE TRUCK AND I'LL TAKE THE WAGON. YOU PICK UP SALSA AND GROFIELD.

I'LL GET PALM AND PHILLIPS.
DON'T WAIT FOR ME.

GOT IT.

GUYS, WHAT'S GOING ON?
ERRK!

WHERE'S PARKER GOING? WHAT THE FUCK IS--
SHUT UP AND GET IN BACK OR I LEAVE YOU.

Wycza couldn't believe his eyes. Of all the stupidities tonight, Edgars' had suddenly taken second place behind Grofield.

GET HER THE HELL OUT OF HERE.

SHE'S COMING ALONG.
PARKER'LL KILL YOU.

THROW HER OUT WHEN WE PICK UP SALSA, I'M TELLING YOU.
LET ME WORRY ABOUT IT, HUH? SHE'S COMING ALONG SO SHUT UP.

THERE'S NO ROOM FOR SALSA.
SHE CAN SIT IN MY LAP.

NO TROOPERS YET.
NO SENSE TELLING PARKER ABOUT THE BROAD.
HE'LL FIND OUT SOON ENOUGH.

P--EVERYTHING'S CLEAR SO FAR. WE'RE OUT OF TOWN, AND NO TROOPERS HAVE COME IN YET.
WE'RE COMING OUT NOW.

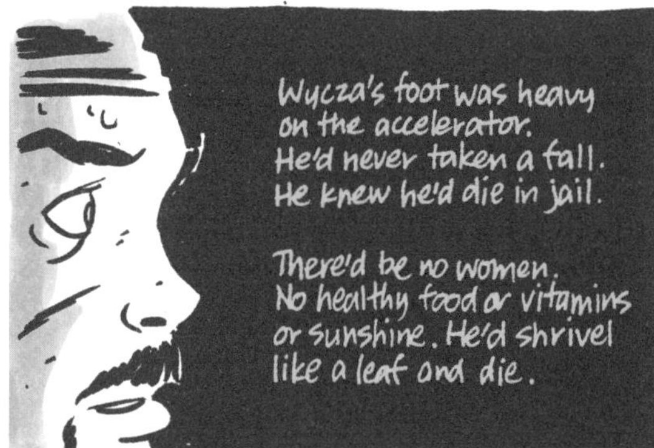
Wycza's foot was heavy on the accelerator. He'd never taken a fall. He knew he'd die in jail.
There'd be no women. No healthy food or vitamins or sunshine. He'd shrivel like a leaf and die.

Behind him, he saw Parker clear the town.

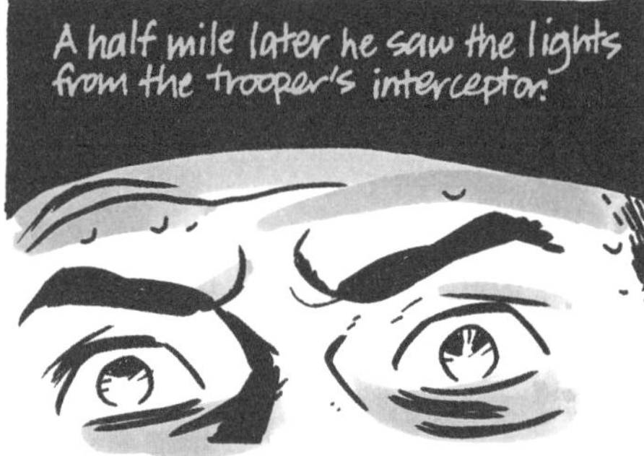
A half mile later he saw the lights from the trooper's interceptor.

The trooper sped past them, toward the blazing town. Wycza felt his boot ease off the gas.
WE'RE CLEAR.

THAT'S ONE PROBLEM BEHIND US.
I'M NOT A PROBLEM. YOU DON'T HAVE TO WORRY ABOUT ME.

WE'RE NOT. GROFIELD IS.

BOOK FOUR

YOU CAN BURY HER DOWN THERE.

FORGET IT, PARKER. YOU DON'T KILL THAT GIRL.

THAT'S RIGHT. I DON'T. SHE'S YOUR RESPONSIBILITY.

YOU DON'T HAVE TO WORRY ABOUT HER, PARKER.
I'M NOT. YOU ARE. IN A DAY OR TWO SHE'LL WANT TO GO HOME.

WHEN SHE TELLS YOU SHE WANTS TO GO HOME BUT SHE'LL NEVER TELL ANYBODY WHAT WE LOOK LIKE OR WHAT OUR NAMES ARE, THAT'S WHEN YOU TAKE CARE OF HER.
BURY HER DEEP, GROFIELD. I DON'T WANT HER BODY FOUND.
WHAT IF I'M RIGHT, WHAT IF THAT DOESN'T HAPPEN?

WE'RE HERE FOR THREE OR FOUR DAYS. THEN WHAT?
NEW YORK FOR THE SUMMER. THEN SOUTH FOR THE WINTER. SHE'S GOT NO FAMILY AND WAS GOING TO LEAVE ANYWAY.
SHE WANTS TO ACT.

SHE'LL GET PICKED UP FOR JAYWALKING AND SPILL THE WHOLE DEAL. SHE'S AN AMATEUR.
I'LL TEACH HER, PARKER. SHE WANTS TO LEARN.

LISTEN TO ME, GROFIELD. SHE'S SEEN US. SHE KNOWS THE WHOLE SCORE. SHE CAN NEVER GO BACK, DO YOU UNDERSTAND?
I *KNOW* THAT. I NEED TO BE SURE YOU KNOW IT.
PARKER, I WOULDN'T HAVE BROUGHT HER ALONG IF I WASN'T SURE.

GO GET HER.

I DON'T WANT YOU LAYING A HAND ON HER.

THAT'S NOT MY JOB. THAT'S YOUR JOB. I WANT TO TALK TO HER.
ALONE.

DON'T TRY TO PUSH HER AWAY, PARKER.

It had been beautiful. It could have been the sweetest and cleanest job he'd ever been in on.
Except Edgars. He'd known, Goddamn it, he'd known all along there was something wrong with Edgars. He cursed himself for not looking into it.

It had all still worked out. Chambers was dead and Edgars was dead, and there was no telling how many locals were dead, but at least they'd managed to get out from under with the loot.
Christ, what a job. One madman tries to blow up the town and another decides to bring a girl along.

GOT THE TRUCK TUCKED AWAY. IT'S ONE HELL OF A WALK BACK UP.

YOU'LL HAVE TO TELL ME THE DEAL WITH EDGARS SOMEDAY.
I WISH I KNEW, DAN.

YOU WANTED TO SEE ME?

PLEASE... THE LIGHT.

TURN IT OFF, DAN.

I NEED TO ASK YOU SOME THINGS, OKAY?
YES.
KLIK

CIGARETTE?
THANKS.
I'LL SEE YOU TWO INSIDE.

DID YOU EVER HEAR OF A GUY NAMED EDGARS?
YOU MEAN THE MAN THAT USED TO BE POLICE CHIEF?
THAT'S THE ONE.

WHAT DID HE HAVE AGAINST YOUR TOWN?
THERE WAS SOME SORT OF SCANDAL. I DON'T KNOW ALL OF THE DETAILS BUT IT WAS A BIG DEAL. HE LOST HIS JOB AND WAS RUN OUT OF TOWN.

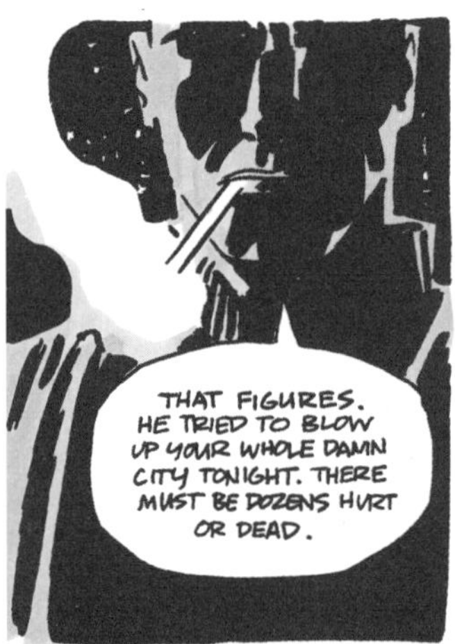
THAT FIGURES. HE TRIED TO BLOW UP YOUR WHOLE DAMN CITY TONIGHT. THERE MUST BE DOZENS HURT OR DEAD.

I MEAN, THE FIRES AND ALL THAT. I IMAGINE SOME OF YOUR FRIENDS WERE PROBABLY KILLED.

BURNING TO DEATH. WHAT A HORRIBLE WAY TO GO.

WHY ARE YOU DOING THIS?

TO SEE IF YOU'RE GOING TO CRACK UP.
WHY?

YOU KNOW MY NAME. YOU KNOW MY FACE.
I CAN'T HAVE YOU GOING BACK AND TALKING TO THE LAW.

THE SIMPLEST THING WOULD BE TO THROW ME OFF THE CLIFF, WOULDN'T IT?
IT WOULD.

WHY DON'T YOU? YOU'RE NOT AFRAID OF GROFIELD.

YOU'VE MISJUDGED ME. I DON'T KILL AS AN EASY WAY OUT. IF I KILL ITS BECAUSE I DON'T HAVE ANY CHOICE.

WHY'D YOU COME WITH GROFIELD?
HE'S MY CHANCE. HE'S SMART AND EXCITING AND PRETTY. YOU CAN TELL HE KNOWS A LOT OF STUFF. HE'LL SHOW ME THE WORLD AND HE'LL MAKE IT ALL FUN.

I HAD TO SCREAM AND HOLLER BEFORE HE'D TAKE ME ALONG, SO DON'T BLAME HIM TOO MUCH.
HE'LL BE IN JAIL WITHIN FIVE YEARS.
HE'S SMART BUT HE DOESN'T ALWAYS ACT SMART. HE SPENDS TOO LOOSE AND WORKS TOO OFTEN. HE DOESN'T PAY HIS INCOME TAX. PLUS, HE'S IMPULSIVE, WHICH YOU ALREADY KNOW.

MAYBE I CAN HELP HIM.

GO TELL GROFIELD TO SHOW YOU WHICH CAR IS HIS. THAT'S WHERE YOU TWO WILL STAY NIGHTS. WE CAN'T HAVE YOU IN THE SHED WITH THE REST OF US.
ALL RIGHT. THANK YOU.

Parker felt the sudden return of desire that followed a job. He was going to need a woman.

Not like Grofield's girl. He wanted something with more abandon to her.
And then he knew who, knew exactly who. Somebody had to tell her Edgars wouldn't be showing up.

FRIDAY, APRIL 24

DON'T TELL ME TO CALM DOWN! I'M LEAVING TONIGHT.
WE DON'T SPLIT TONIGHT. WE MAKE THE SPLIT DAY AFTER TOMORROW.
I DON'T LIKE THIS PLACE, I TELL YOU-
SHUT UP A SECOND. LISTEN--
IS HE COMING BACK?
WHAT DOES HE THINK HE SEES OUT THERE?
NOTHING. HE IS USING THE GRID PATTERN TO SEARCH. THE BACK AND FORTH, YES?
BULLSHIT!
THIS IS BULLSHIT. I'M TAKING MY SHARE TONIGHT.
YOU SHUT YOUR FACE, PAULUS! YOU AIN'T GOING NOWHERE.
ALL THINGS COME TO HIM WHO WAITS.
THAT'S THE TOUGH PART.

SATURDAY, APRIL 25

paulus.

where?
took his car down the hill.
gone to get his share.

THERE'S ONLY THE ONE WAY UP. I'LL GET THE STATION WAGON AND BLOCK THE HILL.
FUCKING PAULUS.

I TELL YOU THIS MUCH; I DON'T NEVER WORK WITH HIM AGAIN.

I MEAN, SHIT...

...IT'S COLD OUT HERE.

THAT SHOULD DO IT.

--SIGH--
WHAT DO WE DO WITH HIM?
I DON'T WANT TO HAVE TO BURY HIM.
SO WE TIE HIM UP FOR A DAYS FEW.
AH - HERE HE COMES.

GET THAT CAR OUT OF THE WAY! I'LL RAM IT!
FORGET IT, PAULUS.

DON'T MAKE THINGS MORE DIFFICULT FOR YOURSELF. COME BACK TO THE SHED AND WE'LL TIE YOU UP A FEW DAYS.

FUCK YOU, SALSA! EDGARS SET US UP TO BE CAUGHT, DON'T YOU SEE THAT?
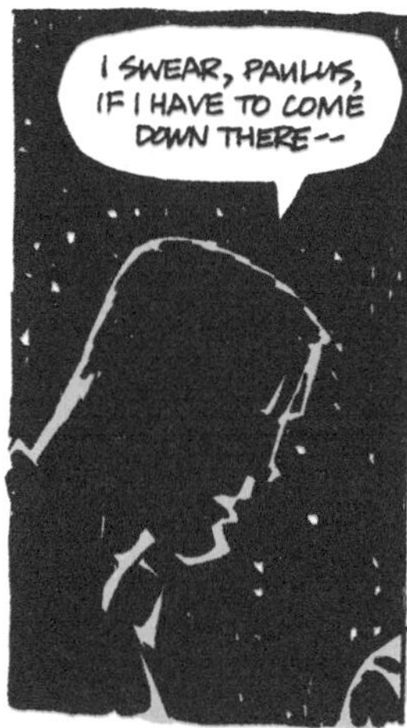
I SWEAR, PAULUS, IF I HAVE TO COME DOWN THERE--

GOD DAMN YOU, PARKER!
WHAT AN ASSHOLE.

ASSHOLES!
LIGHTS

DON'T SCREW AROUND, PAULUS.

30 90 100 120
PRNDL
FINE!

WE'LL ALL JUST SIT HERE UNTIL THE LAW SHOWS UP. ASSHOLES!

WHOA.

PAULUS!

JUMP!

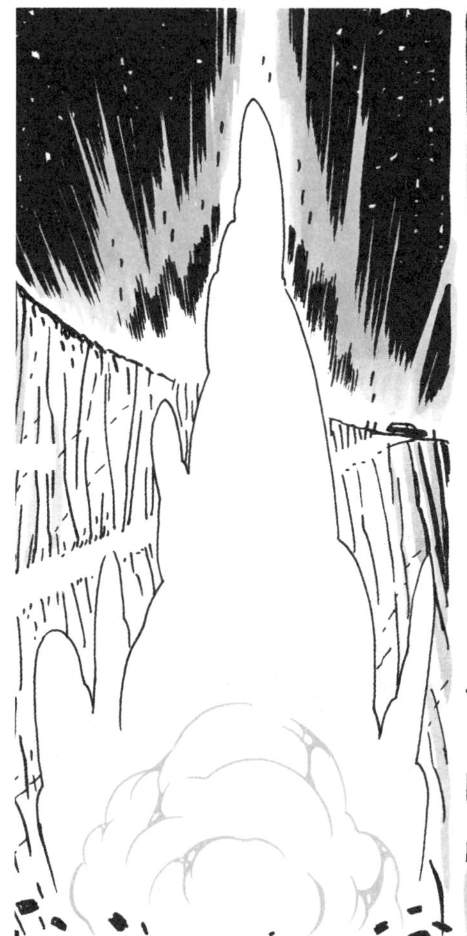

FUCKIN' PAULUS.
HE TOOK HIS WITH HIM.

They'd buried Paulus and the burnt car that night. The rest of the sit was uneventful.
They split the take and lugged the change and guns down to the muddy stream and dumped them in the stinking water.
Pop Phillips set out in the wagon to see if everything was clear.
Cars were packed and the shed was stripped of personal items. Phillips came back to give the all clear.
Each man left with just over $30,000.
Parker was last to leave.

MONDAY, APRIL 27
FICE
401
WHERE'S EDGARS?
HE DIED. OPEN A WINDOW.
YOU MOVE RIGHT IN.
YOU BEEN OUT OF THIS ROOM AT ALL?
WHAT DO YOU CARE?
THAT BIG HOO HAH UP IN COPPER CANYON -- THAT WAS YOU, WASN'T IT? I BET YOU KILLED EDGARS.

EDGARS KILLED HIMSELF.
HE WAS SICK IN THE HEAD. HE WANTED TO BLOW UP THE WHOLE TOWN, AND ONE OF HIS GRENADES BROUGHT DOWN A WALL RIGHT ON TOP OF HIM.
I PICK 'EM, DON'T I? TELL ME, PARKER, WHAT'S WRONG WITH YOU?
THERE'S NOTHING WRONG WITH ME.
THERE'S GOT TO BE SOMETHING, OR I WOULDN'T PICK YOU.
YOU DIDN'T PICK ME.
GET ANOTHER GLASS.
OH, DON'T ACT SO GOD-DAMN TOUGH. WHERE ARE YOU HEADING NEXT?
DRIVE TO CHICAGO.
TAKE A PLANE TO MIAMI.
YOU LIKE MIAMI?
HOW THE HELL DO I KNOW?
THIS IS THE FARTHEST I'VE BEEN FROM NEW YORK IN MY LIFE.

Parker looked at her, and thought of Grofield's girl.
Where do you find one like that?
Forget it, there'd be something wrong with her too.
GET THE GLASS. I'M THIRSTY.
WILL YOU TREAT ME NICE?
WILL YOU FOR CHRIST'S SAKE TREAT ME NICE?
WHY? WHAT HAPPENS THEN?
HOW DO I KNOW?
NOBODY EVER DID. MAYBE I TURN INTO A BUTTERFLY.
LET'S FIND OUT.
THE WINDOWS ARE OPEN!
FORGET THE WINDOWS.
ALL RIGHT.
WHATEVER YOU SAY.

Butterfly,
said Parker.

Sure.

Special Thanks:

James (Phillips) Steranko
Phil (Wiss) Noto
Jimmy (Palm) Palmiotti
Frank (Elkins) Tieri
Dave (Chambers) Johnson
Michael (Cho) Cho
Callum (Wycza) Johnston

and

Abby Westlake
Paul Westlake
Susanna Einstein (of Einstein Thompson Agency)
Ted Adams
Robbie Robbins

PARKER WILL

RETURN IN 2013